PRINCESS ABIGAIL
AND THE WONDERFUL HAT

PRINCESS ABIGAIL
AND THE WONDERFUL HAT

BY STEVEN KROLL
ILLUSTRATED BY PATIENCE BREWSTER

HOLIDAY HOUSE / NEW YORK

For my princess Abigail
and her wonderful hats, with love

S.K.

For the Winter Princess, Marietta, the Spring Princess, Emily,
and Poppy, Princess of Fall

P. B.

Text copyright © 1991 by Steven Kroll
Illustrations copyright © 1991 by Patience Brewster
Printed in the United States of America
First Edition

Library of Congress Cataloging-in-Publication Data

Kroll, Steven.
Princess Abigail and the wonderful hat / by Steven Kroll ;
illustrated by Patience Brewster.—1st ed.
p.   cm.
Summary: Wishing to control the outcome of her father's
hat contest, because she knows she must marry the winner,
Princess Abigail accepts the help of a strange
green lizard from the forest.
ISBN 0-8234-0853-1
[1. Fairy tales.   2. Hats—Fiction.]
I. Brewster, Patience, ill.
II. Title.
PZ8.K912Pr 1991
[E]—dc20   90-39213   CIP   AC
ISBN 0-8234-0853-1

Once there was a king who refused to wear crowns. He preferred hats.

Not only did he prefer hats; he loved them. And not only did he love them; he had a special one for every hour of the day and every occasion.

He had tall hats, short hats, big hats, small hats, hats with wide brims, hats with no brims, hats of brocade and hats of felt, hats with fringe and hats with feathers, hats for breakfast and hats for bedtime, hats for balls and hats for meetings. He had closets and closets full of hats.

One year, when it came time to open the fall festival, the king wanted a very special hat.

He strolled through his closets, trying on one hat after another. Nothing was good enough. "I'll ask my hatmakers to make a new one for me," he said to himself.

When he had made his request, the two elderly hatmakers shook their heads.

"We are sorry, Your Majesty," said one, "we have made you so many hats for so long, we have run out of ideas."

"But what am I to do?" said the king.

The two hatmakers shrugged.

The king was upset. He went for a walk in the palace garden, wearing a striped beret. "I know," he said at last, "I will proclaim a hat contest! Whoever makes me the best hat will marry the princess Abigail!"

Throughout the countryside, mothers began sewing furiously for their sons. Aunts began sewing furiously for their nephews. Long lines of young men began forming at the palace gate, because the enchanting princess Abigail was the fairest beauty in the land.

Meanwhile, Princess Abigail was very unhappy. She did not want to marry just anybody who appeared with a fancy hat. Sadly she sat beside the king and watched as the young men arrived daily with their creations.

A handsome fellow from the other side of the kingdom brought a hat piled high with fruit. "Ridiculous!" cried the princess. A duke from a neighboring village arrived with a hat like a crystal chandelier. "Preposterous!" said the princess. A horseman from down the road appeared with something that looked like a horse's head with ribbons tied to its ears. "Absurd!" moaned the princess.

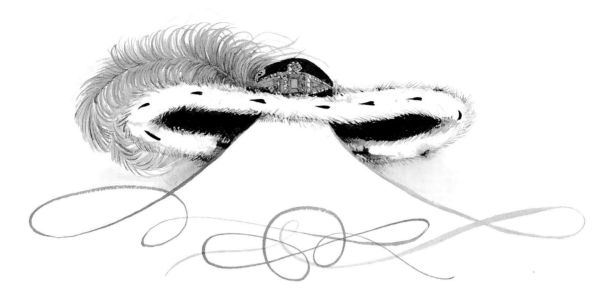

The king turned everyone away until, at last, a prince from a faraway kingdom appeared. His name was Prince Grindstone, and he had traveled hundreds of miles over hundreds of hills and mountains.

He knelt before the king and presented his hat. It was black, with a broad, flat brim edged with ermine. The crown was high, with emeralds and diamonds sparkling at the front. A green plume to match the emerald added a final bit of dash.

The king placed the hat on his head. "Prince Grindstone," he said, "this is not the wildest hat I've seen, but it is the handsomest. I declare you to be the winner of the contest. Rise and look upon Princess Abigail, who will be your wife tomorrow."

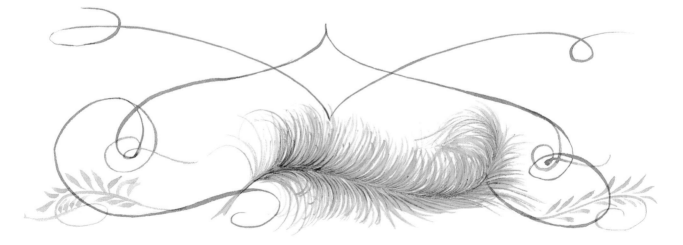

Princess Abigail gasped. Prince Grindstone, though talented at designing hats, was ugly and horrible. He had a puffy, sneering face, tiny, piggy eyes, and huge buckteeth. His clothes were so tight they bulged over his flabby body, and his pointy shoes did little to disguise his bowed legs.

"Thank you very much, Your Majesty," said Prince Grindstone, bowing low. "You could not have made a better choice."

Princess Abigail burst into tears. "I'd rather die than marry such a prince!" she said, and ran from the throne room.

She did not come downstairs for dinner. She sat on her bed and cried, and as the evening wore on, she could hear the preparations being made for her wedding.

At midnight she could stand it no more. She tied her bedsheet to the window frame, climbed down to the ground, and ran off into the forest.

Poor Princess Abigail. It was very dark in the forest, and blinded by tears, she could hardly see where she was going. Stones bruised her feet. Brambles tore at her nightgown.

Finally, unable to go further, she collapsed beside a stream. How could her father make her so unhappy? She cried and cried and could not stop.

She was still crying when she heard a voice.

"Please, Your Highness. Tell me what's the matter."

Princess Abigail looked up—and shrank back in alarm. Before her was a large, wrinkly, green lizard!

"Do not be afraid," said the lizard. "I want only to help you."

"Thank you," said Princess Abigail, and dried her eyes. Then she told him the whole story.

When she had finished, the lizard said, "Do not despair. All is not lost."

He disappeared, but in a few moments, he was back with other, smaller lizards. They brought moss and leaves, and behind them followed a flock of wrens and robins, bringing ribbons of grass and twigs from their nests. Together they began weaving an elegant, handsome hat made of nature, and as it grew, squirrels arrived with acorns, mice arrived with nuts and berries, and chipmunks arrived with bunches of asters.

All through the night they worked, and as dawn came, Princess Abigail saw they had created the most beautiful hat she had ever seen, and the one most perfect to celebrate the fall festival. When the hat was almost finished, six butterflies settled on the brim, saying they would stay in place until the festival had ended.

"I don't know how to thank you," Princess Abigail said to the lizard.

"You do not need to thank me," said the lizard. "Merely return to the palace, and allow me to bring the hat to the king."

Abigail could hardly refuse. She hurried to the palace and climbed back up to her room. She was asleep before she knew it.

Hours later, she awoke to a tremendous clamor. Quickly she dressed and rushed to the throne room.

The king was wearing the hat made of nature. Before him stood the big green lizard from the forest.

"Princess Abigail," said the king, "I have made a terrible mistake. *Here* is the most wonderful hat! You must marry this lizard, not Prince Grindstone."

Princess Abigail smiled a little smile at the lizard. She had liked him quite a lot, but it was hard to imagine being married to such a creature.

One small tear trickled down her cheek and landed on the lizard's head.

Instantly he turned into a handsome prince.

"You have broken the spell," he said. "It was placed upon me by an evil witch when I was very young."

"Oh, my," said Princess Abigail.

She and the handsome prince smiled upon one another.
Wearing his hat made of nature, the king smiled upon them.
Later that day, the prince and princess were married and lived
happily ever after.